Fact Finders™

Biographies

Rosa Parks

Civil Rights Pioneer

by Erika L. Shores

Consultant:
Thomas J. Davis, PhD, JD
Professor of History and Law
Arizona State University
Tempe, Arizona

Capstone
press

Mankato, Minnesota

Fact Finders is published by Capstone Press,
151 Good Counsel Drive, P.O. Box 669, Mankato, Minnesota 56002.
www.capstonepress.com

Library of Congress Cataloging-in-Publication Data
Shores, Erika L., 1976–
    Rosa Parks: civil rights pioneer / by Erika L. Shores.
        p. cm.—(Fact finders. Biographies)
    Includes bibliographical references and index.
    ISBN 0-7368-3746-9 (hardcover)
    1. Parks, Rosa, 1913– —Juvenile literature. 2. African American women—Alabama—
Montgomery—Biography—Juvenile literature. 3. African Americans—Alabama—
Montgomery—Biography—Juvenile literature. 4. Civil rights workers—Alabama—
Montgomery—Biography—Juvenile literature. 5. African Americans—Civil rights—
Alabama—Montgomery—History—20th century—Juvenile literature. 6. Segregation in
transportation—Alabama—Montgomery—History—20th century—Juvenile literature.
7. Montgomery (Ala.)—Race relations—Juvenile literature. 8. Montgomery (Ala.)—
Biography—Juvenile literature. I. Title. II. Series.
F334.M753P3868 2005
323'.092—dc22   2004011100

Table of Contents

Chapter 1

Parks Stays Put

In 1955, Rosa Parks boarded the bus on a December night in Montgomery, Alabama. She walked past empty seats marked "whites only." She took a seat in the fifth row, the front row of the African American section.

Soon, more people crowded onto the bus. They ran out of seats in the white section. Then the bus driver noticed a white man still needed a seat.

Southern cities like Montgomery had laws against African Americans and white people sitting together on city buses. The front rows were set aside for whites. If those seats were filled, African Americans had to give up their seats.

One year after her arrest, Rosa Parks (center) was no longer required to give up her seat to a white man. Her arrest helped change the law.

The driver told Parks to move. She stayed put. She was tired of giving up her seat to white people.

Police officers took Parks to jail. Her arrest sparked a **protest** that changed the United States' unfair laws.

Chapter 2

Childhood

Rosa Parks was born February 4, 1913, in Tuskegee, Alabama. She was named Rosa Louise McCauley. Her parents were Leona and James McCauley. She had a brother named Sylvester.

Parks' father left to find work when she was 2 years old. She did not see him again for many years. Parks' mother took her two children to live with her parents on a small farm in Pine Level, Alabama.

Parks' grandparents had been slaves. They told her about how African Americans were mistreated. They taught her that all people deserved **civil rights**.

Parks was born in Tuskegee, Alabama.
The city is known for the Tuskegee Institute,
a college for African Americans.

▲ In the early 1900s, only white children were allowed to ride school buses.

School

Parks started school when she was 6 years old. In 1919, white children and African American children went to different schools. White children rode the bus to school. Parks and other African Americans had to walk. Children on the bus often threw trash at African Americans who had to walk.

In 1924, Parks started classes at the Montgomery Industrial School for Girls in nearby Montgomery, Alabama. The teachers were white women from the northern United States. They taught Parks self-respect. She learned that she should not expect less of herself just because of her dark skin.

Five years later, Parks left school to care for her grandmother. She also started working at a shirt factory in Montgomery.

QUOTE

"I liked to read all sorts of stories, like fairy tales . . . I read very often."
—Rosa Parks

Chapter 3

Fighting Segregation

For many years, U.S. **segregation** laws had kept African Americans and whites apart. African Americans could not use the same drinking fountains as whites. They could not swim in the same pools.

In southern cities like Montgomery, only white people could ride in the front of the bus. African Americans could board the front of the bus to pay the driver. But they then had to get off the bus and enter again through the back door. Sometimes, the bus driver left before African Americans could get back on the bus.

For many years, African Americans could not share water fountains with white people.

F A C T !

In the early 1900s, it was against the law for whites and African Americans to play checkers together.

Parks was angry about these experiences. She did not think African Americans should be treated this way.

Marriage

In 1932, Parks met Raymond Parks. He worked as a barber. He was part of the National Association for the Advancement of Colored People (NAACP). This group worked for fair treatment of African Americans.

The Parkses were married in December 1932. They lived in Montgomery, Alabama. Parks' husband encouraged her to finish high school. She went back to school and finished in 1934.

Parks and the NAACP

Parks **volunteered** with the NAACP. In 1943, she became the group's secretary in Montgomery. Parks worked for Edgar Nixon, the head of the local NAACP group. Parks wrote letters and set up meetings. She also worked with young people in the NAACP Youth Council.

In the 1930s, many young African Americans belonged to the NAACP Youth Council. ⬇

Chapter 4

Arrest and Trial

On December 1, 1955, Parks worked at Montgomery Fair, a department store where she sewed clothing. After work, she got on the bus to go home.

As more people boarded the bus, the white seats filled. One white man could not find a seat. The bus driver told Parks to move to the back so the man could have her seat. She refused. The bus driver reminded her that she was breaking the law. When Parks still didn't move, the bus driver called the police.

The police took Parks to the police station in Montgomery. The officers arrested her and took her fingerprints.

Parks was arrested more than once. In February 1956, Parks was arrested for helping plan the Montgomery bus boycott.

Support for Parks

Parks' boss at the NAACP heard that she was arrested. Edgar Nixon called his friend Clifford Durr. Durr was a white lawyer in Montgomery. Nixon knew a white lawyer had the best chance of getting Parks out of jail.

Nixon, Durr, and Parks' husband went to the station. Durr paid $100 to get Parks out of jail.

Parks had a choice to make. She could quietly pay the fine for her arrest, or she could fight it in court. Nixon persuaded Parks to take her case to court.

Parks, Edgar Nixon (center), and lawyer Fred Gray (right) went to court on December 5, 1955.

Word of Parks' arrest soon spread through Montgomery. African Americans decided to **boycott** the buses. They asked other African Americans to stay off the buses on December 5, the day of Parks' trial. A group of African American women called the Women's Political Council printed flyers asking children and adults not to ride the buses for one day.

December 5 was a cloudy, rainy day. Still, very few African Americans rode the buses. The white people in Montgomery were surprised.

In court, Parks pleaded not guilty. The judge found her guilty. She was fined $14, which she never paid.

▲ Many buses were empty December 5, 1955. Before the boycott, most riders on Montgomery's city buses were African Americans.

That afternoon, African Americans formed a group called the Montgomery Improvement Association (MIA). A minister named Dr. Martin Luther King Jr. was their leader. The MIA decided that a one-day boycott was not enough. They asked African Americans not to ride on Montgomery's buses until the laws changed.

Parks sat in the front row while Dr. Martin Luther King Jr. spoke about plans for the boycott.

Chapter 5

The Boycott

The Montgomery bus boycott lasted through winter and into the next fall. African Americans walked to their jobs. Some rode with others who owned cars. White women often gave rides to their African American maids.

Many white people in Montgomery disagreed with African Americans' fight for equal treatment. Dr. King's house was bombed. Some whites wanted to hurt or kill Parks.

On November 13, 1956, the U.S. Supreme Court took action. The judges decided segregation on public buses was against the law. Their decision became official on December 20. After 381 days, the bus boycott ended.

During the boycott, many African Americans rode in cars with friends, while the buses stayed empty.

QUOTE

"When people made up their minds that they wanted to be free and took action, there was a change."

—Rosa Parks

After the Boycott

Parks' brother worried about her safety in Alabama after the boycott. He asked her, her husband, and their mother to come live with him. In 1957, Parks and her family moved to Detroit, Michigan.

Parks continued to work for civil rights. She gave speeches across the United States. She spoke to people about the bus boycott. Parks sometimes went to marches to protest poor treatment of African Americans.

◄ On December 21, 1956, Parks was able to choose any seat on the bus.

The Civil Rights Act

In 1964, the U.S. Congress passed the Civil Rights Act. This new law said the government could no longer make laws based on a person's skin color. Segregation did not end right away in all places. But the new law did start to change the lives of African Americans.

After the Civil Rights Act was passed in 1964, Parks still spoke for civil rights at protests. ⬇

Chapter 6

Parks' Legacy

Parks continued working for African Americans. In 1987, Parks and her friend Elaine Steele started the Raymond and Rosa Parks Institute. This Detroit group helps young African Americans learn about the civil rights movement. They learn about Parks' part in the fight for equal rights for all people.

Awards and Honors

Parks won many awards for her civil rights work. She won the Martin Luther King Jr. Nonviolent Peace Prize in 1980. The U.S. Congress gave Parks its highest award in 1999. She was given the Congressional Gold Medal of Honor.

Parks won the Congressional
Gold Medal of Honor in 1999.

25

In 2001, Parks was honored in front of the same bus where she refused to give up her seat.

FACT!

At the Raymond and Rosa Parks Institute, young people teach computer classes to senior citizens. Parks herself was a graduate of the first class.

Cities and colleges also honored Parks. The city of Montgomery renamed the street where Parks boarded the bus in 1955. Cleveland Avenue is now called Rosa Parks Boulevard. In 1998, Troy State University in Montgomery opened the Rosa Parks Library and Museum. It is near the place where she was arrested.

Today, people know Parks as the "mother of the modern day civil rights movement." Parks' strength against racism set off protests that improved the lives of all Americans.

Fast Facts

Full name: Rosa Louise McCauley Parks

Occupation: seamstress, civil rights activist

Birth: February 4, 1913

Hometown: born in Tuskegee, Alabama; raised in Pine Level, Alabama

Parents: Leona and James McCauley

Siblings: younger brother, Sylvester

Husband: Raymond Parks

Education: dropped out of high school in 11th grade; earned her high school diploma in 1934

Major awards:

Martin Luther King Jr. Nonviolent Peace Prize, 1980

Presidential Medal of Freedom, 1996

Congressional Gold Medal of Honor, 1999

Time Line

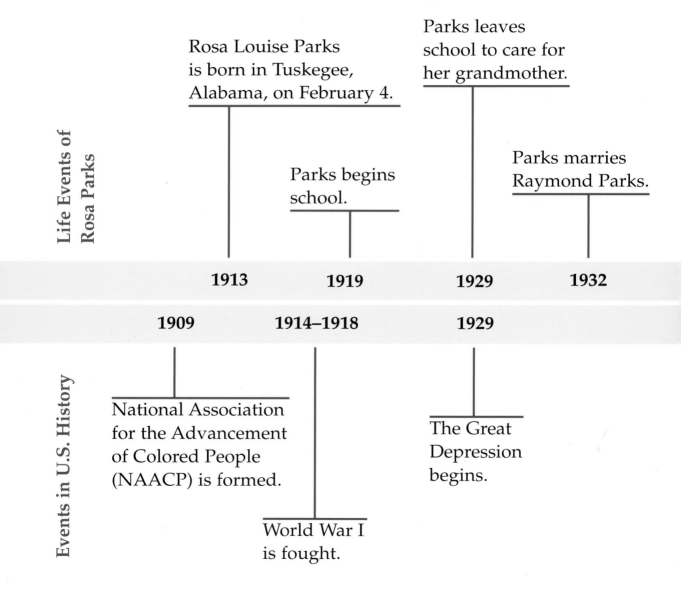

Life Events of Rosa Parks

Rosa Louise Parks is born in Tuskegee, Alabama, on February 4.

Parks leaves school to care for her grandmother.

Parks begins school.

Parks marries Raymond Parks.

1913   **1919**   **1929**   **1932**

1909   **1914–1918**   **1929**

Events in U.S. History

National Association for the Advancement of Colored People (NAACP) is formed.

The Great Depression begins.

World War I is fought.

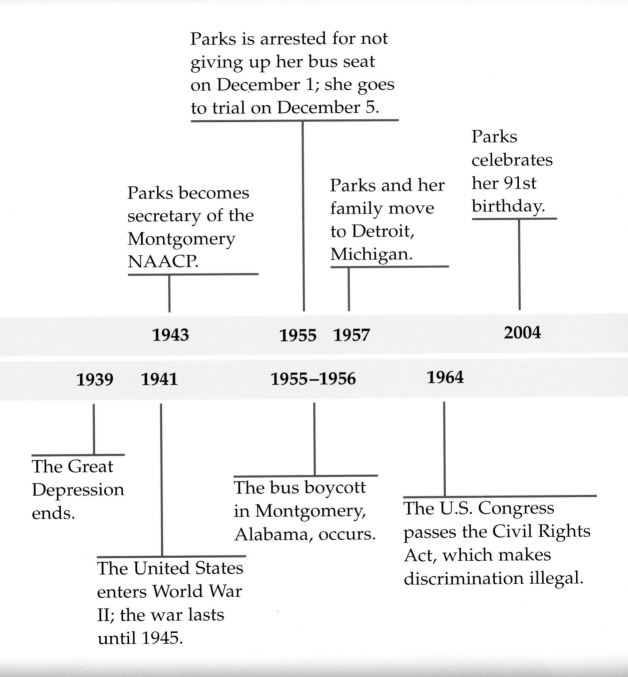

Parks is arrested for not giving up her bus seat on December 1; she goes to trial on December 5.

Parks becomes secretary of the Montgomery NAACP.

Parks and her family move to Detroit, Michigan.

Parks celebrates her 91st birthday.

1943   **1955**   **1957**   **2004**

1939   **1941**   **1955–1956**   **1964**

The Great Depression ends.

The United States enters World War II; the war lasts until 1945.

The bus boycott in Montgomery, Alabama, occurs.

The U.S. Congress passes the Civil Rights Act, which makes discrimination illegal.

Glossary

boycott (BOI-kot)—to refuse to take part in something as a way of making a protest; this refusal is also called a boycott.

civil rights (SIV-il RITES)—the rights that all people have to freedom and equal treatment under the law

protest (PROH-test)—a statement or action against something

segregation (seg-ruh-GAY-shuhn)—the act of keeping people or groups apart

volunteer (vol-uhn-TEEHR)—to offer to do a job without pay

Internet Sites

FactHound offers a safe, fun way to find Internet sites related to this book. All of the sites on FactHound have been researched by our staff.

Here's how:

1. Visit *www.facthound.com*
2. Type in this special code **0736837469** for age-appropriate sites. Or enter a search word related to this book for a more general search.
3. Click on the **Fetch It** button.

FactHound will fetch the best sites for you!

Read More

Dubois, Muriel L. *Rosa Parks: A Photo-Illustrated Biography*. Photo-Illustrated Biographies. Mankato, Minn.: Bridgestone Books, 2003.

Fine, Edith Hope. *Rosa Parks: Meet a Civil Rights Hero*. Meeting Famous People. Berkeley Heights, N.J.: Enslow, 2004.

Mara, Wil. *Rosa Parks*. Rookie Biography. New York: Children's Press, 2003.

Index